DATE DUE

OCT 3 1 2017	
MAR 2 5 2019	
SEP 2 4 2019	
OCT 2 8 2019	

PRINTED IN U.S.A.

Good Luck!

A St. Patrick's Day Story

By Joan Holub

Illustrated by Will Terry

Ready-to-Read • Aladdin
New York   London   Toronto   Sydney

For Molly McGuire –J. H.

To my family, for all of
the love and support.
–W. T.

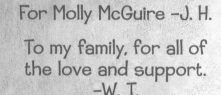

ALADDIN PAPERBACKS
An imprint of Simon & Schuster Children's Publishing Division
1230 Avenue of the Americas, New York, NY 10020
Text copyright © 2007 by Joan Holub
Illustrations copyright © 2007 by Will Terry
Also available in an Aladdin library edition.
Designed by Lisa Vega
The text of this book was set in Century Oldstyle BT.
Manufactured in the United States of America
First Aladdin Paperbacks edition January 2007
2 4 6 8 10 9 7 5 3 1
Library of Congress Cataloging-in-Publication Data
Holub, Joan.
Good luck!: a St. Patrick's Day story / by Joan Holub ;
illustrated by Will Terry.—1st Aladdin Paperbacks ed.
p. cm. (Ready-to-read Ant Hill ; #2)
Summary: While attending a St. Patrick's Day parade, Mike,
Matt, and the other young ants pursue a mischievous ant
leprechaun convinced that he will bring them good luck.
ISBN-13: 978-1-4169-2560-6   ISBN-10: 1-4169-2560-0 (lib. bdg.)
ISBN-13: 978-1-4169-0955-2   ISBN-10: 1-4169-0955-9 (pbk.)
[1. Ants—Fiction. 2. Leprechauns—Fiction. 3. Parades—Fiction.
4. Saint Patrick's Day—Fiction. 5. Stories in rhyme.]
I. Terry, Will, 1966- ill. II. Title. III. Series.
IV. Series: Holub, Joan. Ant Hill ; #2.
PZ8.3.H74 Gol 2007
[E]—dc22
2006010105

"Parade!"
said Wade.

"Green bike,"
said Mike.

"Green hat,"
said Matt.

"Catch him!" said Jim.
"But why?" asked Guy.

"For luck,"
said Chuck.

"That way!"
said Jay.

"No luck," said Chuck.
"A clue!" said Drew.

"Hey, look!"
said Brook.

"Chase him!"
said Jim.

"No ant," said Grant.

"No luck," said Chuck.

"Clue two!" said Drew.

"Up there!" said Claire.
"Get him!" said Jim.

"No ant," said Grant.
"No luck," said Chuck.

"Clue three," said Dee.

"Green ant!"
said Grant.

"Grab him!"
said Jim.

"Climb it,"
said Kit.

"Look in,"
said Lynn.

"Oh, boy!"
said Roy.

"A treat!"
said Pete.

"Good luck!" said Chuck.